*For Norah, John, Patti, Papa and Dee Dee*

Library of Congress Cataloging-in-Publication Data

Spooner, Joe.
  The elephant walk / written and illustrated by Joe Spooner.-- 1st ed.
     p. cm.
  Includes 42 hidden elephants.
  Summary: Norah yearns to be taken for a walk to see elephants, and eventually she has to gently remind her patronizing parents that the zoo is the place to do it.
  ISBN 0-9745686-3-5 (hardcover : alk. paper)
  [1. Elephants--Fiction. 2. Zoos--Fiction. 3. Humorous stories. 4. Picture puzzles.]  I. Title.

PZ7.S76375El 2004
[E]--dc22

2004011208

Cover & Text Design by Aimee Genter

**Arnica Publishing**
3739 SE 8th Avenue, Suite 1
Portland, OR 97202
(503) 225-9900
www.arnicapublishing.com

This isn't one of those *Where's What's-His-Name?* books, but there are quite a few elephants hiding in it. Not counting the ones on the wallpaper and the pajamas, we found forty-two elephants. We could, though, be wrong about that number.

*For Ginger*
*— Joe Spooner*

Written and illustrated by
**Joe Spooner**

Edited by Michelle McCann

arnica
PUBLISHING

One night Norah had a dream, a big dream, a dream big enough to hold an elephant.

The elephant said, "Let's play hide-and-seek. You won't ever find me!"

"Yes, I will," said Norah.

"No, you won't," said the elephant.

"Oh, yes I...." But Norah woke up before she could finish her argument. Norah was a girl who liked to finish her arguments.

"I'm going to find that elephant," she declared as she jumped out of bed.

Norah looked out her window at the blue sky with its white puffy clouds, and said, "It's the perfect day for an elephant walk!"

So she packed up an Elephant Finding Kit—one set of binoculars, one notepad for sketching and taking notes, one first-aid kit (she never left home without it), one elephant whistle, one bag of elephant treats, one elephant net (just to be safe), and one *Elephant Identification Guide.*

She was ready.

Norah raced down to the kitchen and announced: "It's the perfect day for an elephant walk. Let's go find some elephants!"

Norah's parents were used to her plans for big adventures.

"Hmmm... an elephant walk," said her dad. "Sounds good to me."

"Wonderful plan," said her mom. "But there are some things you have to do first."

Norah always hated those "things-you-have-to-do-first" things.

"First, you have to eat your breakfast," said her dad.

So Norah quickly ate her cereal and drank her orange juice.

"We're wasting time!" she yelled, running for the door.

"Wait, wait, wait," said her mom. "Next, you have to brush your teeth!"

So Norah bolted for the bathroom, climbed up on her stool and brushed her teeth.

"Don't you know that elephants like the early morning best?" she said. But it was hard to understand her with her mouth all full of toothpaste.

Norah was nearly out the front door when her dad stopped her. "One last thing. You can't go anywhere without getting dressed."

"Oh... yeah," said Norah and she marched upstairs to her room.

"They're all going to be gone if we don't get going!" she grumbled, pulling on her clothes.

Finally, Norah finished all the "things-she-had-to-do-first" things and they headed out for an elephant walk.

As they strolled through the neighborhood, Norah peered into her binoculars and consulted her *Elephant Identification Guide.*

"Now where could all the elephants be?" asked her dad with a chuckle.

"Oh, they're around," Norah explained. "Elephants are excellent at hiding themselves. You've got to look very carefully to spot them."

"Look!" said Norah's mom, pointing up the street. Norah yanked her binoculars into place. "Just look at that beautiful old house."

"Thanks, Mom," said Norah, lowering her binoculars. "It's beautiful and it's old, but it's not an elephant. We're on an elephant walk here, remember?"

They wandered through a park.

"Spotted an elephant yet?" asked her dad.

"Nope," said Norah "There!" said her mom, pointing up at a tree. Norah looked carefully, but didn't see any elephants.

"Check out that squirrel," her mom finished.

Norah shook her head. "Squirrels, oh they're terrific," she said, "but this is an elephant walk, not a squirrel walk!"

They walked through a garden.

"See any elephants?" asked her mom.

"Nope," said Norah.

"Wow!" cried her dad. Norah scanned the ground where he was looking. "Those are some pretty flowers," he said.

"Yes, very pretty…" Norah sighed, "…for flowers. But we're not looking for flowers, are we? We're looking for elephants!"

"Any elephants around here?" asked Norah's mom.

"Nope," said Norah.

"Up in the sky!" said her dad. Norah looked, but she didn't see any elephants.

"Would you look at that blimp," he finished, "it's enormous!"

"Yes, that is one enormous blimp," groaned Norah, "and that was a nice squirrel and those were pretty flowers and that was an old house!" Norah threw up her hands. "But this is an elephant walk. Where-are-the-elephants!?!"

With that Norah trudged up the sidewalk toward home.

When they reached the front porch, Norah's dad shrugged. "Maybe the elephants just aren't out today."

"Maybe it's still too cold for elephants," said Norah's mom. "Or maybe…"

But Norah wasn't listening. She was having an idea. "I've got an idea!" she shouted.

So off they headed, following Norah to a new location....

# THE AVENGERS

## » BATTLE AGAINST LOKI

Written by
*Tomas Palacios*

Based on Marvel's *The Avengers*
Motion Picture Written by
*Joss Whedon*

Illustrated by
*Lee Garbett, John Lucas,*
and
*Lee Duhig*

Based on
Marvel Comics'
*The Avengers*

MARVEL
NEW YORK

www.marvel.com

TM & © 2012 Marvel & Subs.

Published by Marvel Press, an imprint of Disney Book Group. No part of this book may be reproduced or transmitted in any form or by any means, electronic or mechanical, including photocopying, recording, or by any information storage and retrieval system, without written permission from the publisher. For information address Marvel Press, 114 Fifth Avenue, New York, New York 10011-5690.

Printed in the United States of America

First Edition

1 3 5 7 9 10 8 6 4 2

G658-7729-4-12032

ISBN 978-1-4231-5477-8

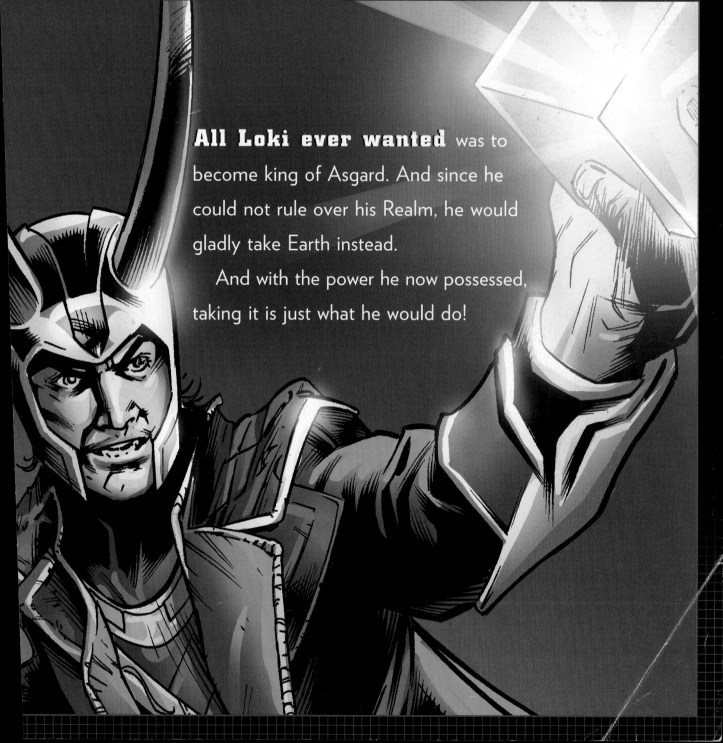

**All Loki ever wanted** was to become king of Asgard. And since he could not rule over his Realm, he would gladly take Earth instead.

And with the power he now possessed, taking it is just what he would do!

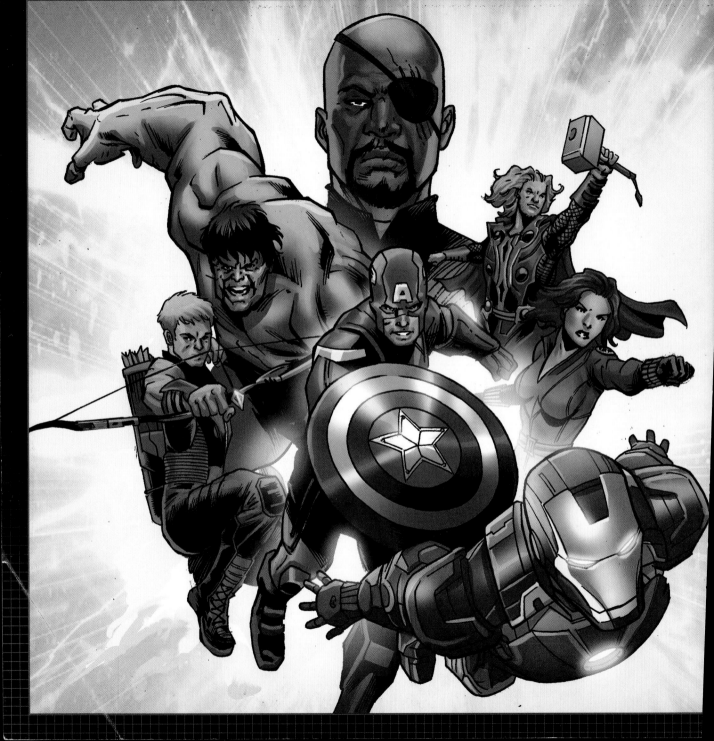

**But Nick Fury, director of S.H.I.E.L.D.,** had other plans for Loki. Fury had been secretly assembling a team of Super Heroes.

There was the invincible Iron Man, the Super-Soldier known as Captain America, S.H.I.E.L.D. agent Hawkeye, superspy Black Widow, and scientist Dr. Bruce Banner, also known as the Hulk! Lastly, there was Loki's own brother, Thor.

By themselves, they were good at what they did. **But together, they were Earth's Mightiest Heroes!**

**And on this day,** it would be their first battle as a team. But it wasn't going to be an easy one. Loki possessed an object called the **Tesseract.** It was an ancient artifact that could be used as a terrible weapon.

The Tesseract gave off gamma radiation, which S.H.I.E.L.D. was able to track thanks to **Bruce Banner.** And no one knew more about gamma radiation than him.

**First up was the invincible Iron Man!**
He rocketed out of the Quinjet toward Loki, ready
for battle. Iron Man used his repulsor beams and
fired them at the Trickster! **One shot. Two shots.
Three shots!** But Loki avoided each one with ease.

Suddenly, Loki fired an energy blast from the
Tesseract. But Iron Man was fast! His armored suit
warned him, and **he dodged the blast!**

**Loki was down, but he wasn't defeated.**
So Black Widow jumped into action! Black Widow
was a master spy and she knew how to fight!

The S.H.I.E.L.D. agent used her martial-arts skills
to clash with the villain. She kicked and punched
and punched and kicked. Loki was quick and
blocked them all.

Then he fired a blast from his scepter directly at
the hero! Black Widow leaped out of the way
just in time!

**It was now time for Hawkeye** to show his fellow Super Heroes what he could do. Hawkeye quickly fired several arrows at Loki. Loki dodged them, and they struck the rocks behind the villain. But they weren't ordinary arrows. **The arrows suddenly exploded**, throwing the villain to the ground. When he stood back up, he saw Hawkeye already firing more arrows in his direction!

**Loki created the illusion** that there were dozens of him to try to confuse the Super Heroes. But the next person he was about to face wasn't just a Super Hero. He was a Super-Soldier! **He was Captain America**!

Cap grabbed his red, white, and blue shield and flung it toward the illusions, collapsing each into a cloud of smoke. Just one Loki was left. The real Loki!

Cap threw his shield at the Trickster. **CLANK**! Loki was knocked to the ground once again!

**Loki had fought every Super Hero.**
But there was still one more he had to face—his own
brother, the mighty Thor! Loki wanted to beat his
brother once and for all.

It seemed as if this would be their final
showdown! Thor hurled his mighty hammer at Loki,
smashing his brother into the mountain.

Angry that he had fallen to Thor once again, Loki
stood and rushed at his brother. Loki's scepter and
Thor's hammer clashed! Lightning shot down from
the sky, striking the villain!

**Finally, Loki was defeated!** All was quiet. The heroes gathered around the fallen villain.

Alone, they knew they were not enough to defeat the powerful Loki. But as a team they had beaten the Super Villain and taken back the Tesseract. **The world was safe once again.**

**Back on the Quinjet**, Nick Fury applauded the heroes for capturing Loki. He knew this team would work, and they had proven that to him today.

But Fury knew that more threats were looming around every corner.

That's why Fury needed one more Super Hero to complete the team . . . a Super Hero that was **big** . . . and **incredible** . . . and Fury had the perfect candidate in mind. . . .

**The incredible Hulk!** The other heroes looked on in amazement as Bruce Banner changed into the green goliath. He was huge! He was even bigger than Thor! With this last Super Hero in place, Nick Fury had **assembled the ultimate team.**

From that day forth, these Super Heroes would
assemble and be known throughout the world as

**the Avengers!**